WATER TABLE

2799-FORE

WATER TABLE

S. Scott

2799-FORE

To order additional copies of this book, contact:
Xlibris Corporation
1-888-7-XLIBRIS
www.Xlibris.com
Orders@Xlibris.com

CONTENTS

This book is dedicated to my husband, Paul;
for without his patience, interest, and technical support,
my poetry would have remained my own but unknown to
those who might find kindred spirit in their verse.

WATER TABLE
BECAUSE COMPASSION IS
THE UNDERCURRENT OF
ALL THINGS

I can't remember the beautiful words that meter my tempo, so each day I must poetize life, for only in musical expression do I live.

I'm never bored in nature but in human company, without conversation in some depth, I'm lost.

I am without destination. My path is the warm face that gives me direction. My days are spent rambling on any road for That, for I am a pickpocket. In the herd of humanity, in the splash of people at the ball park, in the funneled troop of patriot workers en route to their jobs, in the turnstiles of the rapid transit—there amid the somnolence of beach ones, I siphon the unattended spirit. In vacant glances, I pillage from the nectar of every man.

SAGE TODAY

I'm looking for a sage
Have you seen one?
I'm longing for wisdom today
I'm hoping for the eye of Nietzsche in some stranger with
eternity in his gaze
I'm searching for Picasso and Thoreau—not in art but in the
flow of life
Cadence for me is music—elongated symmetry—my calling,
birthright
Now I'm pained but not remiss in my striving
Mind my words: I'll find feeling in this day
Because I'm a furtive wonderer
Seizing Love—Midas magic is my way.

2799-FORE

MAYBE ANOTHER TIME

No time for novel of meaning
No time for the repetitious task
No time to be intimate with a smile from the soul
No time to feel sky in a glance
No time to feel pain for a reason
No time to write letters to old friends
No time to stop still with delight—stoic thrill for the poets who
praised epic plans
No time for loneliness with meaning
No time for crazy bone sad
No time to be
No time to see
How sad
Maybe another time.

S. SCOTT

MUSE IN THE MORNING

The muse comes to me in the morning
But before that I take time to be
As I shackle my step—focus my thoughts—nothingness comes it
seems
The contrasts of life sit like jelly—welling up cosmic grin
Savory and fine
Conundrum fine ineffable that peace from within.

EASY PEARL

Disconsolate my life with this meaning
Charity had scared art away
The cares and worries of others usurped them, preoccupied my days
Forgotten for me were life's struggles
Happy habits screened memories of pain
Did I look to others to share their load?
Vicariously it was pleasure in vain
Lost to me now was suffering
Worthless life seemed without toil
Though my struggles were real
The pearl not so dear
For abated was the friction
My calm's own addiction to rub grain—frenzy pain for my goal.

S. SCOTT

MAGIC CHARITY

Busy yourself with kindness
Giving can yield so much glee
Driving a neighbor's child to school
Their car broken—your yoke comes with ease
To make cozy a home for children
Secure smiles with warm cookies and chat
Norman Rockwell of soul
It's time to be bold
Just do it—it's part of the act
But know when to stop and listen
Write down your thoughts as they come
Give not too quick
Savor the tricks
Magic charity is God's great plan.

FOR MY FRIEND

I'm brought back to life with your memory
I'm really not here as most are
I'm jarred once again with your struggles
Your striving was vision afar
I've traveled the road with great wonder
Though broken and maimed and in doubt
I've searched high and low for my level
Sincerity—my tool and my clout
Now the only thing I can remember
Of the maelstrom and my struggles in life
Is the truth that love feeds all my actions
Diaphanous that feeling of life.

S. SCOTT

TIME FOR DREAMS

A hobby of mine is not talking
Imagine what fun it can be!
The thought of it makes me excited
Dumb for a day with my dreams

No part of harrowing echoes of street-sounds noise of the day
I selectively dip with hummingbird skill to the Honey where
stillness pervades
The quiet of the unexpected where loneliness never prevails
Good cheer in every limb that lingers on languorous chair

It's a wonder—this sense of contentment
In the center of some Cosmic calm
The unity of me
In the unity of we
That feeling of love profound.

BABY SERENE

Have you ever searched into a baby's eyes
Into the innocence that spawns inner call
To the time when pabulum and soft carrots could have satiated
us one and all
To the time when we could be strolled all day rewarded with the
slow pace of life?
Or the time we could kick our feet to the air—refusing the
clothes of life?
A time we were allowed to be naked
A time we could smile all day
A time we could whimper with longing and need and someone
would step in to care
An openness and trust for living
A childlike approach to life
The right kind of creed
Which adults sorely need
Adherence to the rocker—lullaby—carriage saunter
Adherence to baby serene.

EARLY IN THE MORNING

Early in the morning I'm peaceful
My nights are for arduous dreams
At the dawn of the day—the quiescent way has resolved di-
lemma and fright away
Not logical the fairytales and follies
That run rampant in my maggoty mind
In sleeping tryst
The shadow enlists
The taboos I have left behind
I won't fight them
I can't flee forever
Only primitives escape empty fate
Everything has meaning—significance
Insight is never too late.

ELMER BELMONT

I'll never forget Elmer
We talked about Andover and the Brute
I said that love makes the world go 'round
He was suddenly knocked off his feet

We met in Jack London's Museum
I was dusting his legendary books
It was almost like rubbing a genie or awakening a primal nook
A stranger with my chemistry had found me
And I in turn prompted his glance
Our real communication unspoken
A glimmering light flamed honest stance

We spoke of the high and the noble
We rambled for hours on truth
My love for Elmer unfounded
How did our talk recall radiant youth?
No stranger to me was Elmer
Though I met him clear out of the blue
Like a bell—limpid eye—cozy fireside

Elmer—human being so true.

S. SCOTT

TOO FAR GONE

I'm too far gone
I can't live without vision
I can't survive hollow souls
I'm bent on the muse inside me
The probity impossible to hold
Like a cancer of light it imbibes me
Like a secret—a mystery untold
The magic of love is inside me
A feeling an impulse to hold.

SILLY

Silly to talk of achievements
Folly is loquacious man
To be in the now does not allow—memory of sorted sound
Are we not called to make connections?
Sometimes trite but true
The ordinary are only a springboard
A vehicle to friendship renewed
I'm so spoiled
I can't live without insight
Noble thoughts I must constantly pursue
To experience—to know—to realize that glow
I can be silly as long as I'm true.

ZANY AT THE END

I'm serious at the beginning but a zany at the end
Some truth of life absorbs me and I struggle for a blend
So serious is my purpose—I'm pulled out of dream with angst

What selfhood means to life?
What kind of people seem bored?
When spontaneous is synonymous with life?
When kindness relieves aching sore?

The questions are important
I'm as frenzied as a fiend
I pounce on them like thwarted fox
In fables prompting avaricious spleen

My antics are never completed
But buffoonery takes a rest
Not certain I've resolved really anything
Yet gingerbread fills my head.

MYSTICAL PRAYER

I can't imagine my life without You
I can't imagine a day without peace
When the cares and worries of irrelevant life seem to flee in the
down of the geese
Chattering birds in the morning
Bells and the smiles of fine kids
Roses and iris endearing
Wondrous colors and scents
So vivid my world that surrounds me
So steady my toil-thickened hands
So furtive the beams of my eyes serene
For I feel like I've eaten the sun.

NOTHING BUT ME

I love to get up and do nothing
I love to get up and just be
Overwhelmed by a sanctuary of stillness
Overcome by the light which is me
Like a babe I was born to forget life
Drawn to sleep which would hide precious self
But each day song bird call to my innards
To the bird baths—to the wells—to some depths
To the waters that constantly renew me
To the sea of humanity at its best
And the best is the love that connects me
To the river of some greater Self.

ON THE WAY TO GRACE OLIVER'S BEACH, MARBLEHEAD

Meaning springs from me and aches for expression
As the epic poet surfaces,
The coffee house music envelops the ceiling fan
And daffodils shine into me from the window box
I roam outside toward the sensual tulip leaves—green ladies
yawning into Spring
Alluring the flowering plum
And robin's pink breast makes pastel egg to rest on verdant new
blade
Black birds cackle while I romp
And everywhere forsythia brightly invade me
Speckled granite rounds the tar walk
Serpentine my jaunt on broken pavement and fissured road
Eager my appetite for nature
And greedy my thirst for spirited sea and the mellow waters of
Redd's Pond ahead
Winsome the impression of Gingerbread Hill and Joe Froggers,
cookies of youth
I sigh, sauntering down the hill with the feeling of the fluid yet
stationary
I rest on a bed of purple mussels gazing out to Peach's Point

Away from the machine .. calm ..calm
Forever .. calm.

S. SCOTT

HOMILY IN ME

There's a homily in me
Waking reverie
Meaning in life so clear
It's the clear of rainbow bright
It's the clear of shimmering light when August moon gives boon
of warm insight
There's the dawning of the self—tear-stained face that melts in
quest
When great sorrows turn to jest and playful mime
Joyous symmetry—metaphor and me
Is that all? Enough for me
At the end dearest friend
Unity.

DON'T DISTURB THE WILDLIFE

Quiet, you'll disturb the wild life
Whisper, can you hear Its call?
Be ready you know not the moment
Surrounds us the wonder of all
Nature saves us each day—get mindful
Nightingales sing—wind chimes ring

QUIET PASSION

I'm still on the side of passion though older and more aware today
When I'm drawn to the stoic in silence—something in me is
enraged
I've always wanted to be there
Beyond the gropings of life
Beyond the quibbles of married folks
Beyond the 'teen pimple frights
Beyond the chattering name-brand freaks
Beyond the fat-free freaks—

I have liked to fancy the virile with pleasure
To salivate with gourmet delights
To squawk like a duck at injustice
To dream of adventure in life—

Still the coterie of poets enchants me
Literary mystery piques my mind
Life's meaning is deeper and less angst filled as I sally into each
day so fine
But the bother and questions are gone now
Understanding all ideas I don't seem to need
Quiet passion is my memory, my life's vow
Substantial my focus supreme.

RETURN TO RUMI

I woke up this morning with a prayer on my lips
Then villainous life spat on me with lists
Litanies of debts
Unanswered letters
And the unremembered poems of my life's greatest splendors
But I was not sad though busy and witless
For under it all my life's sorted crypt ness
Was the need not to worry but just to be
So I snuggled up with nothing—a time to be me.

S. SCOTT

LOYAL TO HOME

They listened to her person
They watched her true to self
They cursed the ground—her pathway
With spit—vile talk—and stealth

But think they did to know why
This weird one lived so swell
Convert she did with energy
They knew her as themselves.

ETERNITY NOW

Part of every spirit
Breath of all that lives
Glow from every sunshine that comes from grace within
Such a close connection
plant and soil combined
All that's really missing
Is always in the mind.

SHADOW

It's a wondrous thing—the shadow
If you've known it and not feared it—the best
The energy that resides inside it
Can circumvent the soul and then rest
Subtle yet sultry it imbibes one
Like a lighthouse
Like a beacon
Like a strobe
Like an angler who throws his hook to the sea
It's wonderful to feel the unknown.

BE CAREFUL

I wasn't meant to be busy
But sometimes busy earns me life
Exerting myself for others
Fosters tension and creative strife

I always have to measure
Survival in lieu of good deed
Because separate I'm not
Consideration—my thought
To give has always been me

But though common is my love for all others
Almost sneaky the way I can give
I must remember me
My own charity
Or I'll forget my own reverie.

MOODY

Don't ask me to smile if I'm moody
Maybe a stoic's that way
But I am filled with passion and whimsical folly
Channel feelings another way

Don't think I'm lazy for brooding
When some gingerly snap into life
Many get busy when downcast
While I'm silly trying to figure out life

But sad or forlorn or dejected
No matter the gesture of face
Real feelings have to be answered
Not always with jovial face.

COCKTAIL PARTY FOR ONE

I made my own cocktail party today
A party of one and that was O.K.
I had tried other parties with several, I mean
But they all were horrid they turned my spleen green
There's something hipped, something phony
With those Toulouse-Lautrec characters
Caricatures lonely
I wanted "real"
I wanted "meaning"
So I drank of my own libatious feeling
For hors d'oeuvre I pondered the writings of Mann

The best success—this party of one
I didn't solve problems but I localized one
Boring—vapid whatever you call it
When you make meaningful connections
It matters not who's there
It matters only that you thought it.

S. SCOTT

BOOK OF NOTHING

I read from the book of nothing today
Glorious that feeling of happy disarray

On the mother's face as she radiates to child

Something glows from the guileless lover

Someone sings to the hallowed clouds

Some wine brings radiant smile

How very strange and hard to measure—the real the true
Define that treasure

Diaphanous plane
Ineffable pleasure

The limpid—pellucid
Gaze of forever.

"TO BE OR NOT TO BE"

I sat round-shouldered in the rose garden
Perplexed beyond feelings
I knew so much yesterday
I knew nothing today
The roses were comely and sweet
I whispered to them
We humans are different from you
You must feel the sun and rain
We must know to feel o.k.

I AM A CONVERT

I recognize myself as an inconsequential speck of the universe
In my glimmering insight I feel as one scale of the God-fish of life
Not even one—a flash—a blink—a half-thought
I'm floating now inside
Inside
It all happens there
In the mind
The reveries which connect our lives
That give us peace about the great Sun Power
The Loving Unknown for whom we feel Everything.

HOW ODD

The man has brought me down today
As I floated in space in lands far away
As I recreated slums for play
As in my mind were vast sun rays

A baby shows that floating reeling
The darkest schizos dread the feeling

He was heavy and stump like-weary
There I was the one who hovered
With hummingbird and butterfly flutter
He spied me then to pull him out
Those wings of mine he made his clout

And now I'm grounded but heaven bound
The constant yearning keeps me spinning 'round.

S. SCOTT

RETREAT

I love the retreat of morning when slumber has whispered away
Mountains and suggestions of problems
That clutter, reverie of new day
My knapsack I carry with wonder
Reminiscent of vagabonds of old
I intend to collect every spirit I can
In diaphanous song and poem.

SOMETIMES

Sometimes you can't do anything but pray
Lift your heart from weary fray
Storms that beat—that wrench in sleep
Leave mantra on your chattering teeth
Too many people—no time to think
No time to feel your aorta beat
Martha's work—forever servant
Wait on people—purpose not fervent

Silent movies—Hallowed times—Prayers connect vibrating minds.

S. SCOTT

SHOULD

It's so easy for routine to take the day
Blot out pictures of loved ones far away
Dispel the feelings of peace deep within
Distract from the cadence of our breathing—flowing wind
Erode reflection of all in life that's good
Discount the poetic valor of the should

Love takes us beyond all things and then
Puts us back inside ourselves again.

VISITORS IN SEARCH

I don't need distant effusive praise
I need nothing but my silent daze
Reverie—compassion—venture
To make them one is my big adventure
Charity a mere beginning
It ends in love of quiet being
Resilient in patient quest
Dedicated to all searching guests.

S. SCOTT

WONDROUS CITY

Is there reason to like the city?
Is there reason to care for those sounds?
Mixture of car honks and bus brakes
Garrulous beggars and johns
The hotsy-totsy of Fifth Avenue—trendy bars and fancy salons
Sidewalks gum and wine stained
Hopscotch on dead streets
Broken pavement—littered ways
Pigeon droppings—police on beat

I love the city
There is spirit there
Wondrous—wondrous—struggles and cares.

SUGAR TIME

Everyday I say there will be no cookies
Everyday I plan without sweets

Marzipan and chocolates—what use are they
When my heart seeks a different meat?
Milk Duds and bonbons at Showtime
Snack bars on the beach

Coney Island carameled apples
Licorice—the vine ones—red, sweet

Sugar cane and apple strudel
Taffy—cotton candy and the like

I'll take a cookie, no need for caffeine
Insatiable my love for sweet life.

S. SCOTT

HELP

Can I help you with that?
Make you some tea?
What about coffee?
There is one scone left; "please take it"
And now for my pleasure, the silence of me.

ENNUI

Ennui Epiphany for me
Catharsis unfold
Water table of gold
Holy Grail uphold
Mandala of old

equanimity, equanimity

Love is the soul-Soul of the whole.

S. SCOTT

POPPYCOCK

Sometimes life's like a spinning top
Like a whirlpool of empty poppycock
We busy ourselves like rabid squirrels
Hiding our nuts—burying our skills

Who are you?
Who are you?

Connecting is what we're supposed to do

Take the nuts and make a roux
A sauce for life
A gravy rich
Cover all with happiness.

ADORING SILENCE

I didn't do anything today
In the eyes of the world I was dazed
Pickled I thought with the rarest of thoughts
Peace was my body's grenade

It's wonderful that feeling sublime
When earth seemed a virtual gold mine
Thoughts rare to man
Abstract the brand
So vivid
And yet how few understand?

S. SCOTT

LUMMOX

I didn't do anything today
I sat on a stump—felt like clay

I didn't get started
But inside like a rocket
I fondled my energy, my rays

Sometimes emptiness and lethargy we need
From great artists we recognize the seed

The superior do blend
Take their time—great their end

To create
Godly pleasure—self-made man.

REGENERATE

I didn't do anything today
I got up and sat in a daze

After many days of words
Life seemed absurd—but in quiet I regained my gaze

I nestled with silence awhile
I listened for bird calls then smiled

I pulled in my head—breathed and felt fed
From a solitude which seemed to be dead.

S. SCOTT

AT HOME

I never met a friend like the friend in me
In quiet reverie—I feel that me
Some call it soul.
Some psyche
Some self
But I know it well when I feel myself.

RICHARD CORY

Do you remember Richard Cory?
Fatal victim in poetry of the past
Lonely character of misconception
With the problems of the world on his back
Well, Richard Cory is a way of thinking
When we're doomed by others' views
When happiness seemed we don't know where
'Cause inside we can only feel blue
Lonely seems a natural feeling
When connected there's no hollow space
Know who you are
Connect and feel tall
With image no human disgrace.

S. SCOTT

NO FOOD TODAY

I'm living on my fat today
I need to fast for a stay
A period of time to settle my mind
To rotate and re-find my way.

Life a matter of uncovering
Responsibility—an art when defined
To be true to the you
Whether sanguine or blue
While alive
Hidden goal to renew.

COMPETITION IN ME

I compete with myself for meaning
I race with myself within
I beat in some band
Rummage through sand
Search random eyes for a clue
For a genie—some power within me
For a stick Excalibur-sized
For a voodoo to undo
For a spell to subdue
Magic feat
Fable beat
Feeling one-Won.

S. SCOTT

SACRED LIFE

It's sacred to me the morning
When night has awakened to day
When dream and the myths of all men
Have melted into reverie of my way

I cannot live on yesterday's glow
I can't remember another day's grace
I can't remember that feeling of light
That feeling like a spiritual mace

Each day I begin with some longing for the land which is my
own place
I long to remember ripples on the sand
Which the seas eternally erase
Long to be free of duty
Civilized cares of life
Long for the sound of a lover's words
Echoed in the sound of night
Long for my own awareness
Long for my own idea
Long for the blend
A feeling inkling
Long for that Friend Sacred Life.

LIFE

I love to be part of the lowly
Then to dine with the erudite at night
To work with my hands in littered streets
Then read and be part of night
To see rainbows in the gutters around me
Feel ideas tamed with arduous life
Scrub sidewalks clean and then
Savor the gleam
Wondrous Sun
Which brings them all to life.

S. SCOTT

DISCIPLINE

Discipline is part of the path
Part of ritual
Safety against chance
But for me discipline is just time to wait
For the butterfly while he flutters
For the rose that hugs the gate
For the happiness perched bird like me
For the charm that calms all life
For the meter that stirs inside me
It's a bridge
A feeling bright.

ETERNAL CHARM

You beckon me like ear to chime
Like eye to sea
Titmouse song of early morning
Yawning cat
Languorous moments
To feel beginning
To earn the day
Beauty surrounds us in many ways.

S. SCOTT

WHEN

When to dream
When to wander
It's so much fun when it's not a bother.
When to wait and when to wonder
When to work and what to ponder
When to start—when to finish—
When to make propitious wishes
When to smile—when to be serious
When to trust the doubtful mysterious.

VAGABOND DREAMS

Vagabond is a wonderful word
It's a Charles Kuralt word
It's a wandering word
Perspective from a moving train
To exotic lands
To intriguing planes
Walking stick along track beam
Head bent down to rippling stream
Airplane high in billowy cloud
No return for quite awhile
Vagabond beneath a tree
Vagabond a word for me.

S. SCOTT

FOR GOODNESS' SAKE

What do you do for a living?
What's your profession in life?
You say you're a human being
Strange answer some kind of device?

Are you hiding?
What supports you?
What's that . . .what's that you say?
The litany you now give me sounds weird in this world of today

Take only what you need for living
Be sincere—pay whatever it takes
Be kind—It was kindness that sent you
Feel love in each dubious face

There's a kernel of peace in all things
Compassion can help connect
Those who control are not enemies
But wannabes insecure in unrest

It's bogus to think you can know everything
Eke out life as it comes and become
Do the right as you see the right of Lincoln
Precedent for all those to come

Just remember, win or fail, nature comes back
Sunshine finally rises for day
Find Joy in each waking moment.
Find goodness for goodness' sake.

TRAITOR MOUSE HAND

The traitors today are the watered-down dead
With styrofoam hearts
They dream without pledge
We get instead computer-heads
Prolific with nothing
They speed ahead
Fast with morals
Slow to think
Nobility bores them
Literates stink
What about those with passion? Who can feel?
Who have compassion?

The angler's gone
His Fish—dead bait
Religion now is to be Bill Gates.

VACATION

Vacation for me is to go with the flow
To orchestrate music of my own inner glow
To be with people endearing in depth
To be peaceful with my dreams in a world often vexed
To walk with my saunter that's languorous me
To sop up all nature from flower to tree
To savor the life-style of all things free
To relax with my aura, with the intimate me.

S. SCOTT

TAME

Control the squirrel!
Busy tail stir
Control the clouds
As tornados they whirl
Harness dam of water broad
Stop the bird with twigs and sod!
Home she makes for her brood to come
Instinct they call to protect their young
Only humans with spiteful control
Castrate bodies—minds—and souls
Seems Intuition tells better when
To help mind-heart—the measure—blend.

THE THINGS THAT MAKE ME HAPPY

The things that make me happy
Give me pleasure and past youth
Are the joys that keep me viable of past memory and the truth

The feeling for a childhood food that's lost its flavor now
The knowledge of a new word can empower with the Tao
The morning sun
The moon at night
The glow of self-expression
When sincerity and way of life
Combine in one's profession

Forever young—an attitude
For everyone a pleasure
To feel the good in all of life
Gives happiness forever.

GRAND FINALE

Each day can have grand finale
Each day laborious life
Wearied from novel of merit
Exhausted with valorfull strife
To work to be thorough with something
Each heart has its own inner plan
To realize life—make a statement
Sometimes indolence can give mindful hand.

NATURE'S LOVE, WRITTEN AT BOW LAKE, NEW HAMPSHIRE

Beyond the grimaces of men
The curt and morose
The furrowed brow and tightly-pursed lip
Beyond those who holler and grumble—screechers of doom
Ugly those sores of ego fetid with scorn

There in the menagerie of unbandaided grief
Loving salt preserves a memory—retreat
The Valium of the waters that flow from the stream
St. John's Wort of the lake and chamomile sea
The ripples on lake more than Materhorn of chocolate
Coat jagged innards—java my spirits that saunter
Down to the pond of new day and I slumber
Awake with lone dove's call.

S. SCOTT

PARK BENCH

I love the park bench in me
Quiet reverie
That reminds me of mother's words
Take small bites
Eat life right
Breathe a lot
Sigh insight—with the meaning you find on your way
Bring vacation to each day
Wake up slow—yawn with praise
Life's a trip—treasure hunt
Find the perfume in the skunk
Just sit down—find that park bench today.

NOTHING

In the quiet before the day
Subtle silence metered my maze
Deep in the land between waking and sleep
Far from the slumber of the mundane deep
There in the tunnel—path of my soul
The stillness of nothing resides and is bold
While parades of spirits whimsically stroll
Saunters the heart in promenade unfold
Virginia Woolf and Heraclitus
The Tao of now—the gold of Midas

To hold this still as part of day
To hold this still—such a Way.

　　　　　　S. SCOTT

FESTOON

I don't want to forget the feelings I've learned
A night spent in rapture
A gloaming
A moon
So I conjure up a festoon Martin Eden Style
Draping all those wondrous words
In mind—garlands for miles.

INTUITION

Intuition tells you when to stay
Linger with the sunshine of another day
Poke along like indolent puppy
Conjure dreams unlike the yuppies
Of greater goals and grander themes
Of being bold with self-esteem
Intuition tells you what to connect from angry eye and limpid pest
There is feeling there in those spaces
Unprogrammed—undated
Probity that paces
Intuition reminds us of our home within
Intuition is love and visceral being
Intuition is wisdom—the reason for living.

S. SCOTT

ETERNAL FEELING

I can't imagine night from day
Reverie my eternal way
Love of now and Love of never
Expecting something to last forever
Special feeling inchoate—still
I hold it now both angst and thrill
A better potion you'll never find
Love is the grandest state of mind.

UNDERTOW

Drowning with anxiety and doubt
Tension in family—strangling clout
Much like the sea—stormy me
Raging my spirit as insights flee.

S. SCOTT

NO REASON

No reason to feel this way
Part of the breeze and the fray
Chaos and banter
Chit-chat and slander
The natural—affected—all bray
In the morning the chatter of birds
In the day the cantor of words
They all come together the wicked—the feathered
And give me this cloud
Earth haze.

CASTLE IN THE SKY

My dreams stand above the rubble
My hopes hover over the clay
Broken glass gives me kaleidoscope
To imagine a grand new day
How strange there are those bleak and lonely
Morose whether poor or rich
My dream is to live in a castle
Quixotic of mind enriched
My mission is to dream life together
It's a joy and a wisdom to hitch
All the sordid and sadness around me
Exquisite my happy niche.

S. SCOTT

COFFEE

Everywhere coffee house Schubert
Hissing foamy milk
Busy ambulating people on track to work
Sounds not subtle compete for thoughts timid with night
In need of whispers
Brisk all others

Be still my insides
Be patient
Tenaciously hold to rooted tree-branches pulled by hurricane
Anchor ship flogged by raging storm

E-mail is not forever
Feelings of the Eternal are forever.

ON FOUNTAIN PARK BENCH, MARBLEHEAD, MASSACHUSETTS

Here with hill breeze
Maple leaves flutter with gentle wind
Shimmering ripples surround Gary's Island ahead
As a lone pine silhouettes the sea
Chopping and helicopter sounds at bay
Morning rays and bird calls
Celebrate new day.

S. SCOTT

ENOUGH TO SAY

Sometimes I can't think of anything to say
All I can do is feel the day
Feel the love of a passerby's eye
Feel the care of a door held wide
To allow me first entrance at the postal station
To allow me a greeting from a well-wisher's patience
The dilatory smile
The countenance of the beagle
The slow cup of coffee with endearing people
How can I account for—explain ?
The pleasure was mine
That's enough to say.

QUIET CENTER

There was no place to hide
No mountain nor beach
To siphon emotions, embellish in speech
Commit to paper as my very own beat

Perspective I needed
Distance—removal
So I stepped inside me to a nook marked behooval
Behooved to be quiet
To focus on center
The eye of Calm soon soothed me together
Seems a raging storm was slapping my boat
Now my glass-bottom focus allows me to float.

SOMETIMES

Sometimes you can't do anything but pray
Lift your heart from weary fray
Storms that beat—that wrench in sleep
Leave mantra on your chattering teeth
Too many people
No time to think
No time to feel your aorta beat
Martha's work—forever servant
Wait on people—purpose not fervent
Silent movie
Hallowed time
Prayers connect vibrating minds.

TAO

I'm tired of this crap
I wanted Nobel Prize
I get rap
An empty beat from hollow minds
Dripping with beer—debauched with wine
What about the urge to be
The noble quest—the myth unseen?
It's there I know though imageless
Taunted by machines and embellished in unrest
Festering in me the need to be
To imagine something more than needs.
Or maybe needs are inner life
Not bulging biceps or computer frights
Well I don't know—I can't say
But I struggle to feel the Tao in each day.

S. SCOTT

SORROWFUL MOTHER

Take my arm
Take my leg
But don't take my children—my heart away
Don't take their minds that have not become
Don't take their dreams which are yet to come
Don't replace hopes with digital tombs
Or Internet craziness worse than witches on brooms
Don't take their souls like Faust for a whim
But leave them indolent for a time within
Time to idealize and recognize heroes
Time to be part of the native ritual
Time to see tree and sky with a nod
To foster Intuition
The Wisdom of God.

OUT OF SYNC

Someone said you're out of sync
He furrowed brow at me
You think you damn Romantics are majestic as the sea
You think the august sky and oaken-ashen tree
Give you your roots like Indians who say "thou" for everything
You think the world is sacred
You wander without lust
You splash into the gutter
While your head in clouds adjusts
You're out to lunch he stutters
The world is not like that
In crooked stance I mumbled
The world is what I make it
In reverie and task.

DIFFERENT DRIFTERS

What is the difference between drifting on line or drifting in
your head?
Random facts of Internet or
Imaginative dreams instead
Instinct is for primal man
Intuition godly wonder
Guitar string plucks at primal cord while
Machines they race and plunder
Inane hearts without a clue
Surround the world with gloom
Preach that men are violent and the world is damned or doomed
Books they haven't read a one
Grand masters found a bother
Odysseus to the Christ figure
They take their lot as pother
But the emerald doesn't lose its green if no one cares to note
To be aware Aurelius knew
True drifter is provoked.

RIDE TO THE SEA

Calculate garrulous bird banter?
Sun mellifluous and gay
As it flows into the window
Rhythmic cars in disarray
While whining cat begins new day

No matter
No pother
As wood to chair
As rhyme for rocker
How natural to flow
To breathe and to saunter
Down to some stream
In sailboat to ponder
Where fear and expectation cease to be
Just part of the current
A ride to the sea.

PEYOTE WITHIN

Peyote in me my mystical theme
To feel without drugs
The chemistry of me
And me is my symbol
My life driven effort
To see the cross—Mandala
Eternity in effort
Constrained—contorted—Guernica in motion
I'll never stop striving to see good emoting
To try to decipher
To mellow dual me
The friction the vision
Beyond lotus tree.

SACRIFICE

I don't want their bodies
I want their minds
I want them to settle in
Eternity's time

Problems and dreams
Nightmares they seem
Earthquakes that crack life's stream

But my face is free
People smile at me
They don't see
My tears in my prayers
My every impulse in compassionate care
My awareness of the dome—the stained glass—the cross
They see only a stumbling
Vagabond—lost.
That's how it is
When you suffer for us
What's in it for me?

Wisdom and loss.

FEELING SWIMMINGLY

Around me sullen butterfly youth
Wings held back
Faces not happy nor sad
Inchoate life
Without the sun and sand
Though the sun and sand are everywhere

Not searching, the bellied, bosomed, scrawny-legged old
wrinkled happies
Pursuing naked tots, meandering Tristans, on the sand and sea
Imperfect all
Lost popsicles to the sand
Warm root beer—cold dogs

Indescribable Equanimity.

ASPIRE TO TRISTAN

I don't always feel like Tristan
But Tristan I aspire to be
To float in my own direction
Feel fate as a warm summer breeze
For me life is inner adventure
Compass drawn to feeling of ease
A visceral sport of wisdom
A congenial tack of calm sea
Drifting in any direction
Wandering without notion of shore
Viewing without need of progression
Unity forevermore.

S. SCOTT

ANGRY

When I'm feeling angry it forces me to see
Lets me put my foot down on path uniquely me
Lets me find adventure in swamps of dead and blind

The mediocre eases
The raucous of tongue
The dolt-like empty characters—hooligans and bums

Beyond the fish are heroes
Beyond black sea great depth
Beyond the call a sacrifice
Arduous—Bliss—the bent.

STREET-WALKER

My bliss is the street and the throng of its people
In cities
At lake fronts
Under quiet church steeples
It is there in the middle of some magic calm
The collective of all
Breathes life to my song
My poem, my myth
My journey, my hero

How wondrous
To ambulate on mines
Counted zero.

S. SCOTT

DIFFERENT NOW

It's different now—I remember me
It used to be I could remember everything
A clean shiny washing machine
Dresser bureau spotless
Corner webs—not a one
Litanies of people I could recite with pleasure—their goals—
achievements
Do-dads of measure
Ready for inspection
Furtively pristine
Now I take my respite in feeling serene.

ONE

It's all there in the nothingness of life
Eternal mask
Beyond vision
Mandala
Peregrinating in Halloween gown
I'm a ghost—wholly ghost
In need of nothing but nothing
Giddy the feeling
Woe to confront
To barter
To argue with
To lust for
Maybe passion ?
Of course compassion
I'm One.

S. SCOTT

MANSION

I dreamt of a mansion inside me
In the background a dappled sky
Wondrous this vision—Utopia
Everything synchronized
The rooms all interconnected
The grand rooms musically flowed
Like one body interdependent
Grand waltz of a giant composed
Magical this sanguine portrait
Of a land and a sea in me
Grandiose and august the feel
Between dream and reality.

SMILE ON AUTUMN

Be still for awhile
Tea leaves in your smile
As autumn's red maples parade

Steal out to the sky
Where bright
Stars mount your eyes
In reflection of those far away

Feel warm squirrel's advance
Feel his spirit in his prance
As he zigzags with zest hiding nuts

It's a wonderful array
Hayrides—apple trays
Scents of cinnamon-sticks in cider fume the day

Count the chestnuts you're been dealt
Think pumpkin pies of wealth
And be stealthy for your health

Settle down—hibernate
Find the wonder on your plate
Turnip taste—don't you waste
Fall's way.

BLISS

I call to you with a quiet voice
Sometimes screaming
From dreams
From the eyes of those on any street who smile at you as member of the club
From the undercurrent of the soul black and white
From the voice within that says, "No, this is not me."
From the words and letters—songs and poems that connect your idea—your ideal
From your enemies who help define your anger
From your wanderings in gutter to summit
Among the lowly, poverty stricken and rich
Away from mediocrity and comfort
A struggler for joy
A sublimator of pain toward something grander than yourself
A knower of passion and compassion

I am your bliss.

BIRTHING

No more chatter—frenzy
Clear a place on the table and let me be
Want to look on shiny wood—feel it
Let me think awhile on that
Let me pull it apart
Put it in one stack—then another
Inside a drawer—on the floor
Forget it
Walk with it
Hold it to the light of day
Shutter with it at night and pray
Dream on it
Confirm it with a slap
From the mystery of imagination
It comes—loving magical persuasion

A poem is born.

RUBBISH

I can't remember the history of Russia
Nor the plots of Shakespeare
Nor my dimwitted numbers
My memory serves me in another way
It sings child laughter on the street
It rings of church chimes a constant beat
It pulls my leash with golden retriever
It helps me splash with birdbath fever
On crowded ways and bustling fairs
The zest of life
The souls of cities
I remember only some illusive meaning
To understand all was not the feeling
The trouble is it's hard to say
Wondrous the rubbish remembered each day.

MANDALA

It's a mystery the circle within
To have meaning without understanding
To habitat with life
Feel wonder—delight
Unflinching with cogent fright

Dream on between friction and strife
Make story with your own inner sight
Make sense of this world
Though all seems absurd
It's a feeling
Mandala—sun bright.

S. SCOTT

VIATICUM

The "petites madeleines" and kiss of mother
The tea-stained cup
The tea-bag wonder
How simple ritual meets soulful dare
To hold the mystery of magic care
Sacrament and sacramental
For sacred life we long to share
Touch of doily
Scent of spice
Fond remembrance of childhood ripe.

LASSO

There's a feeling you get on a warm sunny day
A feeling that comfy will invade for a stay
Homey with sweet scents
Kind memories parade
Pilot fire inside
Something good on the way.
A feeling you'll freeze it to savor the thrill
Part longing, part wonder, part peaceful, the drill
Spirit of mind, glad to lasso
Serendipity on High—alchemical that too.

S. SCOTT

PLATE OF SKY

Are there too many things on your plate?
Then why not eat of the sky
Float like clouds with dappled grace
That yearn for space on high
Burrow in the wild bird's down
In fleece of lambs at rest
In sloping fields wild flowers yield
By sunbeams madly fed.

Don't be greedy for more things to do
When weary body sags
Lift your mind rainbows to find
In dreams to rest, renew.

FRIENDSHIP IS CHOCOLATE

Weary with a friend can mean sharing welkin sky
Otiose on the couch or eating chocolate pie
Telling of your dreams or dreaming side by side
Not to give a faugh for how they spell or drive
Probity is there
No matter looks or breed
Sharing of yourself
What a happy deed!

S. SCOTT

HUBRIS

You are looking like a mushroom there
You live your life in selfish care
It's sad you know—you arrogant—self-centered
You miss so much—Narcissus rendered
Imagination has better clout
It gives to all
Redeems from doubt
To see as one
Us lowly folk
From gutters—rainbows
From wonder's route.

PATIENCE

I can't be fast
I must feel the moment
The sensuous tree's bough
Its whirl in motion
To skirt the sun
Van Gogh proportions
To drink the sky
August the notion
Imagery and elocution
They float by like magic potion
Lemon-drop in teacup pond
To hibernate with inner song
Breathe with wonder
And be involved
It's a trick you know
That Dharma call.

It gives to all
Redeems from doubt
To see as one
Us lowly folk
From gutters—rainbows

CREEP

Creeping into silence
What a happy task!
Stillness in the moment
While cars soar and pass
The stars
The moon
The firefly
How calm their beckons bright
How deep the depths
The soul at rest
As world just rolls right by.

KITE SO DEEP

I'm fighting the list today.
Do this
No I won't
Haunts my head
For my mind wants to dream
The mythical to deem
To register the ineffable unseen

I'm thinking of the skyscrapers at night
Close to their Mondrian lights
White squares on black
Seems the contrast
O'Keefe's New York comes into sight

I saw for the first time a friend
In her eyes
The same kind of blend
She was there but unseen
Now we lingered
With shared dreams
It's wonderful to be separate
Yet blend.

S. SCOTT

Duty didn't help with this tryst
But the ritual
The litany of lists
Was a path to me
A bridge it seems
To launch my kite high
So steep.

MORNING GLORY

Forget the night
When wilts my bud
My pistil slips as residue—as mud
Stuck it seems with vapid day
When thoughts are stagnant and minds, they stray
The wicked time when doubts shatter
The dreams of sleep and happy matters
The mending time
The catalyst
When stars define
And passion's bliss
When is it that life seems fine?
Morning glory is my time.

S. SCOTT

BLAKE'S DREAM

Dreams purse my lips in the morning
Mingled with prayers and the night
Closer to the truth
My heart in a loop
Mandala—tornado of light

The chimes in my neighbor's back yard
The rain splash on streets—gutters—cars
The slippery barrage
A festoon—collage
Between reality and bliss—how bizarre!

Then the wind spat the rain on my pane
The cat's paw reached out in hungry pain
Stentorian sound of the clock's alarm
Brought me back to my duties plain.

But I knew I was safe for a time
Scribbled words took first place in my mind
The sacred unseen
Played some harp to my spleen
Knighted porcupine
Aura magic—Blake's dream.

PLAY

It's a beautiful kind of ray
When the stars and the moon meet day
A shimmer in the soul
Leaves the heart quite bold
With adventure
To search a new way

Silhouetted chimney on sky
Lights from inside fainting by
Dark comes to day
In whimsical array
It's a marvel
When the mind's at play.

S. SCOTT

MOKSHA AT THE END

My motor gets started with pain
As I trip over cat disdained
Breaking from slumber
Like a babe slapped with wonder
I leave dreams
For desires unclaimed

People who cry out in need
Emotions that scream for esteem
They plunder my soul
Oh let them go
Beatrice I'll invoke with gleam

It's sneaky to escape ways of pain
Furtive the eyes beam the game
Walk through the flame
Truly lotus unclaimed
Moksha—illusive the strain.

PICKLED

Cheerful serenity and loving kindness
That's all there is at the end
Nobody's there
You're one big stare
Pickled with insight and ware
Your glass bottom boat which once was afloat
Searching with issues in mind
Lies in abeyance—achieved or depleted
Tabloid your mythic behind
The anchor's deep
Now in retreat
Did you make it, the heroic find?

Oh well—ishcabibble
The cat and the fiddle
Can you feel it,
That Oneness sublime?

S. SCOTT

CURIOUS

I'm not there anymore
In the argument
Heated debate
I fight and make scenes
But it's bogus sheen
The veins and the adrenalin that shake

I'm not here anymore
With the bombastics
Cacophonous querulous fools
Fool a man? No! I'll be damned

If I act any different than I am.

GANESH

It's the elephant's way
Slow and prolonged
The sway of his body
The obstacles gone
The twitch of a friend
The bow of a tree
The gait of someone
I've known also as me
The smile of the sanguine
The furtive beam
The cozy contentment
When for most
All seems bleak
Of course you say
It's the time of day
Burgundy warmed
By your own simple way
A coffee in morning
A cordial at night
When knowledge and habit
Make respite of life
In the sway of the elephant
In his pendulum of life
I feel I am One
No obstacles in sight.

S. SCOTT

FOOLISH WAY

Be careful when you are feeling too happy
Be careful when you're riding too high
Remember elation of past moments
Like tornadoes they quickly whirl by
Forever euphoric is tempting
Gripping cheer we can wallow in all day
Be aware of dreams steeped in pleasureful extremes
They can turn
Sometimes odious that way.

SHADOWED FRIEND

I have a friend
I call her that
She says mean things from the top of her hat
At first I felt hurt and vexed
For my poems and dreams she held in jest
But then I realized she was low
Without insights she stayed below
She fiddled with the loud—sarcastic
Designer clothes were her great classic
While I the bumbling free to fromp
Wandered around, sincerity my trump
It's good for me this kind of bogus
I reaffirm my truth, my focus
I hear my friend in loving beat
I search her beauty beyond skin deep
She pokes me
Jabs me voodoo fashion
I must not squirm but feel her passion
For understanding can stretch our hearts
Prove glamour shallow
For love's our lot.

S. SCOTT

GOD'S STRIDE

I want to recognize feelings
To describe so as to stand in awe
Whether putrid—odious or magnificent
To see them with heart that's all
Those directions of spirit elude us
Chimeras like tumultuous sky
Whirling Van Goghs of passion
Those secret shadows of ours inside
The conscious
The mindful
Lie fallow
Like the blind with their dogs and sticks
They patiently wait
For the sounds we call bliss
And they ride
Just short of
God's stride.

OUT OF ORDER

Disarray and out of order
Maddens mind and wracks the bold
Contents strewn
Selective rubbish
Where are glasses
Valued lists
In menagerie and rubble
Separateness and
Out of place
We have time to sort our feelings
They come first as part of fate
When the mind is out of order
Circumventing
Whimsy bound
There's a time and place for all things
Synchronizing is how we're found.

S. SCOTT

BIRTHDAY RUBBLE

Sitting in the pile of wrappers
Salutations and birthday cheer
The iris of your eye accepts them
Their trappings rubbish
Their thoughts sincere
When at last you meet
Those rich years
Scribbled notes
Trump the bold
When cherished memories
And friends' elixirs
Become champagne of inner soul
Past follies drift like comic wonder
Your silly life and wrinkles bold
Suggest that we are all quite simple
In some eyes
That Oneness glows.

SENILE

Have you realized how happy you can be
Though you fumble at check stands with ease
There's a grin in your soul
Recognizing you're old
And realizing the cheerful in serene

Loquacious to all—tellers sigh
You forget doggie bag and stroll by
You're not in the race
Last place is your fate
You thank God for no pain—worries slide

Rapport seems part of the plan
Connecting with all things—poem grand
Embarrassed—what's that?
It's all in the past
You seem pickled without vintage flask

Your birthdays all turn to mirth
Your bright eyes speak of past worth
Age not the test
When quality rests
Senile is truly rebirth.

S. SCOTT

MITZVAH

Retrieve the smile when mitzvah happy
When symbols of great knights aren't old
When grail or chalice supports your wonder
And mystery like magic snows
A fleecy white
A down of glory
Trombone of feeling
Reverberates self
The simple joys
The heart that's singing
Chattering memories
In cheerful stealth.

ORCHESTRATE YOUR FALL

My fable is rich to discover
Sunshine in harrowing day
How many look high to billowy clouds
As Van Gogh with heartfelt praise?

The maple trees tall
Their gold freely falls
Flutters so joyous the drift
Clutter for some
While wondrous the ones
Who feel magic alongside life's rifts

Then sigh with your dreams
Faint without scream
The poison is ambrosia disguised
The falls and the tears
Of society's stares
Impervious to them you glide

Why not float to your end
Like the leaves' nimble bend
Orchestrate the falls in your life?

S. SCOTT

DON'T KNOW YOUR PAIN

Maybe I don't cry when you're crying
Maybe I don't bleed when you're torn
Maybe I don't flinch with the pain you have
When some lance seems to pierce your soul

You're right, I can't feel your suffering
My blood stays in fated self
But I have known pain
Life's moaning refrain

Compassion speaks for itself.

SEE US EVERYWHERE

Was I nearing death? I saw the one
The face of blind man past
I heard the laugh of joyous us
When all hearts' love did last

The spirit of strong character
"To be or not to be"
Was not just quote of Shakespeare
But bible—family tree
Rich or poor the inner score
To tally virtue true
There was no question
What is beauty
Or what was inner truth

They're just a bunch of feelings
But when they're everywhere
Are you old?
Or just old soul?
I see us everywhere.

S. SCOTT

INTIMATE PURPOSE

When I wake to the depths of black morning
Inspiration still sleeps in abyss
I trust in the night
The stars fondled bright
Can elicit from nothing this tryst
Clairvoyant beyond expectation
Sanguine beyond normal paths
Ecstasy is me
Beyond symmetry
What wonder this miracle
Please last!

PEARL IN ME

I used to think some flowery cosmos
Was there beyond the clouds
Or miles away on some display
Of statues with Botacelli smiles

The gargoyles atop cathedrals
Gold domes on steppes afar
Furtive smiles on those you know
When really you don't know at all

The sacred could not be named
And can't be named today
Imagery is all we had
And all we have today

Of that cosmic wonder
Of that Pearl unknown
Pardon me
Not to blaspheme
But part of that Pearl is me.

S. SCOTT

ABSENT MINDED

Absent minded is not really absent minded
It is minded somewhere else
Where dreams connect
And legends rest
"Out to lunch" with the very best
Heroes for all seasons
Valor everywhere
Collective Consciousness of sacred meaning
DNA of inner self
If virtue is our meaning
If goodness is our lot
Those we consider not quite there
Maybe minded
With auspicious plot.

COZY LIFE

Cozy of inner feeling or
Cozy of comfy abode
Peace within when placid rings
Bell of inner control
Not the control of order
Fastidious—tidy or pristine
Aesthetics rests on inner vest
Coat—of—arms of inner esteem

When roses grace inner table
When incense ritualizes life
When your heart can sing
Around the odious and mean
Isn't that truly cozy of life?

S. SCOTT

FLOW WITH THE SHOW

Not there with the unjust and critics
Not there with the querulous and profane
Not there with tears or gearing sneers
For atrocities and displaced pain

But there in the movement of living
Spying on happiness found
The wrinkled pose of a puppy dog's nose
The eager in the beagle hound.

Energy is a strange commodity
Happiness seems to flow
But those possessed with worries and frets
The dismal—they're stopped from the show

The show is how to harness life
The bitter and the sweet
No matter what's unjust
Turn travesty to feat.

MUCH TO DO ABOUT NOTHING

Don't need them now
Intrigues and plots
Seedy suggestions
Excitement to shock

Wannabe nothing
That's me to a T
Accomplished in dreaming
My own reverie

My race is inside
If a race you can call it
My mind seeks some joy
New feeling in a sonnet

There's a rhythm and a stillness
Both things in me combined
That make my every effort
A song, a wave, a shine

For the race is merely show time
A travel anywhere
Wisdom of a lifetime
Takes awareness—Cosmic tune.

S. SCOTT

TO BE OR NOT TO BE

The problem with me is I just like to be
Appreciate the feeling when my eye sees the sea
The smell of a rose
The sigh of the lover
The pop on champagne
The breeze warm with summer
Most of my time
I furtively search
To snatch chocolate from wonder
Grand Marnier of new birth.

ANGLER'S JEST

It's not as if I want not to smile
Be jovial—playful
Find joke in all trials
But living takes an angler's smart
Know when to pull on the fish line—an art
What to pull at
And what to let go
And sometimes
It's hard to smile as you go.

S. SCOTT

LITERATE SPIRIT

Orchestrate your feelings as you orchestrate your way
The literate of spirit need time for mind to play
Interact with beauty
Profound thoughts every day
Find meaning in all virtue
Make lists along the way
Patience is the same as love
Kindness is love too
It's all been said in Corinthians
And don't forget to pray
Take goodness from some evil
Channel if you can
Find sun's rays in all disarray
Seek stillness in parade.

TRIVIAL PURSUIT

In these wide-open spaces
Cacophony and mad' races
Perfidious, odious and bleak

People lose their cool
"Hurry up you little fool."
On the road they explode
Anger breeds

Petulant are we
Bombastic little bees
We are pests
Unaware of the trees

The sylvan slows us down
Welkin sky moves us around
While nugacity leaves only trivial pursuit

We can ameliorate
Turning querulous to quixotic fate
So if you must participate
Find some good in every place
Don't be bare—unaware
Just get started.

S. SCOTT

RUN—PULL—STILL—KEEN

Where there is light
There is shadow
Think it out
And don't be narrow
Will to know
Will to wonder
Open up that heart in slumber
Slave to nothing
Dharma bright
Cosmic wisdom
This is life.

CAMPBELL BLISS

I need sanctuary for life's rhyme
Space to rebuild
Make tryst in mind
At this time
Can't file my nails
Can't dust a shelf
Or clean a pail
Can't tackle endless bills
Or enlist my wits for mail
"Excuse me please
I must be with me"
Stew with time
That's my line
Patience a clue
Stew—then be still.

S. SCOTT

HOLIDAY

Spent the whole day just
Saying its gloaming
That magical lyrical time
When rafting with myth
You fall or enlist
Into wonder and dance with your kind

Alice and Dr. Zeus are the youngers
While the elders are Huxley and Blake
They swirl you along
Mystical the ground
'Til your head is in magical mace
It's nice for a day—a vacation
A free-be—the creative space
When you awake back at home
You're cheerfully alone
But connected with all of your race.

NOBEL PRIZE

Thank God
I'm not noteworthy or conspicuous
Thank God
I have no movie star charm
Thank God accolades don't follow me
Purple heart
Nor armies of spies

To get away with unremembered kindness
To give inauspicious way
To practice some good
Like Robin Hood
Hidden treasures
How furtive the prize!

WHEN I'M GONE

When I'm gone
Please consider my ditties
My verses have some feelings for me bright
Though my drawers a disarray
Household projects in decay
Wordy festoons were my garlands of life

Don't doom me
With my closets of old memories
Dried old flowers from some wedding of the past
A chipped piggy bank
Maybe European stamp
From adventure
I took money
More than bank

Ludicrous are my holey undies
My shelves
How unlacey they be
When they cart me to the morgue
The jocular can be bold

Bequeathed clutter
Eccentric—this character—of old

SMOGGY PEOPLE

Have you ever been around smoggy people
Like a horror ride at amusement park?
Unexpectedly they hurl
Odious shocks—venomous pools
While you're stunned 'cause they're
Friends wielding tools

Some say they screw you over
While others say they're dumping on you
Your emotions shriek
With heart-open beat
Yet your blood does not leak
Though it scars

Skirting the dung of a dear one
Who betrays you
With falsified heart
Acrimonious his way
Outrageous—you're prey
To his villainous jealous-filled plot

It all dissipates when you realize fate
Feelings understand if they know
So go on as you are
With Wisdom's bright star
But be aware of the gifts from black heart.

S. SCOTT

ETERNAL CHARM

I'm dangling here like a weed in your sun
Like marionette in solar play
Dancing with life—zapped with your rays
Nacreous the luster-pearl glaze

When Charm comes from heaven
When magic resides
In the rays of some Cosmic Wisdom

Then Charm lasts forever
Not fleeting its measure
As you wallow and dance with Its Praise.

LOVE IS SNEAKY

Love is Sneaky
Pull it by surprise
Pluck it from smiling strangers as you bask in their bright eyes
Find it in the crazy world—a unity is there
Beauty in squalor you can find 'most anywhere
Goodness centers evil
Decipher it in mind
Retrieving love is pleasure
For the stealthy, healthy mind.

S. SCOTT

COSMIC GUY

Nature's happy
You know why
Never separates from Cosmic Guy

Gulls and pigeons
Dogs and cats
Clouds and rainbows
Imagine that!

Petty gossip inane plots
Roads away from our inner lots
The will to me
I'm a happy camper
Desire for things
Leaves lonely trappers.

"LET THE DEAD BURY THE DEAD"

Step around gloom of the angry
Step around merde—mind crap
Step around pain and those who complain
Like you'd navigate around frightful rock

Be fluid and float in your reverie
Regenerate with sun and stars
Necessity is bare
For possibility we should care
Adroit seekers
Remember the plot.

PRE-MEDITATED ME

No problem
No problem
I'm me
Me generation to a T
Yoga in tune
Self-centered—a boon
When complete
I can give
As I should.

Self-centered is not such a bad word
If that self can connect with the whole
Separate first
Then try rebirth
Meditate and see
How you flow.

HAIR SALON GIRL

There was a girl
With a parlor curl
Right in the middle of her forehead
And when she was high
She was very very high
But when she was low
She was horrid.

S. SCOTT

TURN TO SKY

Attitude is atmosphere
Healthy mind the place
Bend with tulip
Turn to sky
Be bird's flight in space

Nature never lonely
Only fools are that
It's all inside so realize
Look up
Sky helps with that.

JACK LONDON SAILOR OF WORDS

I love to play with words
They conjure up spirit in me
Like Jack London's clothesline in Martin Eden
Words prompt imagination to see

Adventure in scrabble and puzzles
Crosswords front or back
Curious ouija board those dictionaries
Heaven—thesaurus—repast

Sagacious and witty how awesome
Ennui is not for me
Words like gambit and metaphor
Launch mind into portentous sea

Empower yourself—articulate
How rich is the vibrant mind
Awake and aware how interesting
"Can we talk?" Conversation is free.

S. SCOTT

HOMO FEELIA

Cut me and I bleed
But no scab nor scar you'll see

The blood just opens up and flows
In compassion's cosmic sea

It's not so strange to avoid life's searing
Yes, logical to protect your life

But humans leech
Like mosquitoes they reach
And suck from your suchness—your might

The key is to know how to replenish
Love's open heart, trust all souls
Though it smarts when it's jabbed

It has to bleed—that's the plan
Die and elate
Centimeters—open gates
Epiphany—diaphanous—grand.

MILLIONAIRE—IDEAL-AIRE

My winter home is the right hemisphere
Summer home the same

It's balanced there—resort-like peace
Imagination on holiday

Don Quixote—monarch
Guardian muse at home
Ideals in place to operate
Agendas of the great unknown

Metaphor is magic
Myths and rituals too
Probity the lesson
Something you should do

It's real you know
Though invisible
The gold along your path

Be foxy now
It's free to all
For this sinecure dream
Come true.

S. SCOTT

COME UNION—
COMMUNION

Don't just stand there
Do something kind for people
Lonely people
Meals-on-wheels people
Been-there done-that people
Next
Next
Next
Without the nuance—ambience—fatuous connection

Come union
Communion

CATHOLIC

I'm a practicing universal
Looking where east meets west

Trying to find mystical in each moment
In the digital as we progress

I'm not so sure I'm part of progression
But new insights I'd like to achieve

Universal to me
Swimmingly
Dharma babe
Ubiquitous that's me.

And there
Do something kind for people
Lonely people
Meals-on-wheels people
Been-there done-that

S. SCOTT

MAGGOTY LOVE BUG

Love bug—a maggoty worm
Fantastic thought that too
It needs some surreptitiousness
To feel what you can do

'Cause people think you're crazy
When virtue piques your time
"What's in it for you?
What's in it for you?"
It's enough to blow your mind.
Well I like to stop for raindrops
I like to play in the sand
I like to give the shirt off my back
To a vagabond
Adventure in hand

So if I seem too passionate
Frenzied with my life
I'm in it for me
Go jump in the sea

Fantastic that maggot
Love's bite.

ATTENTION

He only did miracles to get our attention
To get us to think as we talk

To balance the conscious
To tame the animal
On the tightrope of life—our lot

Folks can be rancid and stink to high heaven
Hypocrites of beauty they walk
While cripples serene marred yet pristine
Are innocents who thrive on their thoughts

"Your sins are forgiven
Stand up and walk,"
He said it in one calm breath

The end of this story
Kind goodness His glory
The Man who died on our cross.

S. SCOTT

SUBTLE MIGHT

Part of the sacrament
Not part of the Church
Part of the ritual
Which gives me rebirth
Part of the mystical, magical union
Epiphany for now
And hope for more fusion
Breaking the boredom
Taming insight
Connecting with all things:
Eucharist might.

NEBULOUS STILL

Don't forget treasured feelings
Accountable debts of the soul
Bills and the taunts of real life
Circumvent like the merde on the road

Take thanks for your own happy being
Expect not nor judge not at will
It's subtle the nuance of happiness
If you find it, then listen and be still.

S. SCOTT

LOFTY INTRIGUES

Intrigues for the lofty
Heaven bound there
Wandering amiables
In wonder—no cares
Vacation with nothing
But the bright glint of eyes
Sanguine the happy go ambling by
Drunk with the flight of the gull's easy soar
Stunts of free children—their penchant to roar
Be like the tiger
Act like giraffe
Share the existence of supple repast.

GRATITUDE

Can't stand to live without beauty
Praise of your incredulous forms
Thanks for some awareness
Of the comely by the common unknown

Amazing the winsome around us
Spirit in all things unique
Flowers on table reminders
Piquant their aura so sweet

How sad the lonely surround like dust
Without beauty how can they live?
No wine, no tea nor shopping spree
Is complete without your Bliss.

S. SCOTT

DEEPLY REMEMBER

It's hard when engrossed in labor
To remember kind vision of morn
Intentions to live with that inner peace
In the marketplace—today's trendy store

Surrounded with all things so useless
To eke out some spirit of truth
Dam together from well—find the meaning in hell—
On this earth search for love in the dell

Soar deeply into the stars of heaven
Breathe softly with the dawn's crimson bright
Tread lightly—feel the stillness within you
Be close to the Source's Magic Might.

NO BAGGAGE

Let's go on a trip without valise
Briefcase a pother too
Jump on ocean steamer without trunk of worldly roux
Intrigues are such a bother
Parsimonious have more fun
If you're frugal with the cares of life
There's lots more time for sun
Wonder and trust essentials—satchels for your back
You'll find if you travel without baggage
Your cargo is truly first class.

S. SCOTT

PILGRIM'S ROCK

After a labored evening
Of friends projecting vain plots
Creep back into the masters whose vantage point
Have given us those deep and rare thoughts

Those who have suffered the world games
The trivial by imitation wrought
How skillful the genius who circumvents
To hold on to his Pilgrim rock

Be glad if you're part of mean world
At home with the suffering low
For ecstasy can be through discrepancy
To separate first then to Glow.
Ambition to Wander

I wanted to wander today
Revisit old books—valued play
Leisured intuition
Fun with ambition
To wander and saunter away

Away to the call of adventure
With London to Alaska's frigid cold
With Woolf—nebulous aura of woman
With Campbell—a myth to unfold

Gibran showed me love that transcends all
Charming words to administer days
Disobey any who tarnish valor
Thoreau's hero: Be your poem in each day.

S. SCOTT

EXCUSE ME

Excuse me I didn't mean to disturb you
I'm really just trying to see
Not to distract nor perturb
From the symmetry that I long to be
When subtly I can maneuver
Through back street—alley and way
Give my fate up to chance
Ride by-ways to glance
At faces both stormy and gay
I'm really just here to discover
The aura in all things today
Please carry on
It's all quite profound
Don't mind me
Intuition is my way.

BREAKING THROUGH

There's great pleasure with no facade
Nor penchant to masquerade truth
To search for mobility sincerity and kindness
What better grail to pursue
When to a limited measure
One can live life's metaphors
What better epiphany—
That mindful pleasure
That wonderful breaking through?

S. SCOTT

MILITANT BEE

Do you struggle to remember new insight in past day?
To see with your heart as the Little Prince would say
To slow to the whisper of some inner self
Who nudges and prods you to think for yourself
Be stubborn and listen to the muse in your song
Ideal in all effort—the weak and the strong
Subtle are the nuances that suggest grace within
Connecting all nectar from brash to sanguine

Be militant bee determined to take
Ineffable joy from wherever the place.

MUCH TO DO ABOUT NOTHING

Don't need them now
Intrigues and plots
Seedy suggestion
Excitement to shock

Wannabe nothing
That's me to a T
Accomplished in dreaming
My own reverie

My race is inside
If a race you can call it
My mind seeks some joy
New feeling in a sonnet

There's a rhythm and a stillness
Both in me combined
That makes my every effort
A song—a wave—a shine

For the race is merely showtime
A travel anywhere
Not an end but a journey
Cosmic knowledge of those aware

S. SCOTT

Wisdom of a lifetime
Accolades of visceral pursuit
There is much to do with nothing
I'm a wonderful recruit.

PROBLEM

The problem with me is I just like to be
Appreciate the feeling when my eye sees the sea
The smell of a rose
The sigh of the lover
The pop on champagne
The breeze warm with summer

Most of my time
I furtively search
To snatch chocolate from wonder
Grand Marinier of new birth.

S. SCOTT

PIZZA LADY

Beautiful gypsy at play

Swirling pizza in your flamingo way
Piquant Ruben—Oh maybe
Your lips ruby lady
Nurturing bosom your maternal display

Ambrosia of living your yeast
In manna you skirt us with peace
Taunt us your might
Round cheese of delight

Existential your feeling of life.

BEGINNING DAY

I have a game to play
Before birds whimsically prompt day
Before their chirps
Before the burst
Of roadsters on their mundane way

Dilatory with thoughts I wonder
Stray to a stillness that won't stay
Struggle to savor its mystery
Before chimneys are darkened by day

When light silhouettes yawning sycamore
When resurrection is seen in stained glass
When libation is inner elixir
When reverie allows it to last

Meshing the new with the past grace
Conjuring up joy anew
Fostering insight of beauty
Letting intuition be you

Then onto the game's finale
Parcheesi of soul there the tryst
It's all activated by Love knows what

I'm inchoate without my bliss.

S. SCOTT

INTUITION

I'm a mystical maybe
Are you mystical too?
Always a little too far fetched
Pygmalion of the sky that's true

We mystics in clothes are romantics
Mouths open a gap at the sea
Turgid our pupils at dawning
Tearful those eyes with gloaming's breeze

We drink of the spirit around us
Our senses become Midas bright
Seeing with loving perspective
Intuition keeps our Hero in sight.

COSMIC PUDDING

I can't live without cooking together
The knowledge I glean from each day
The snapshots of life like the smile on a friend
Or a stranger turned friend in some play
It's rich this gravy—this compote
Farrago with splendor of all
Bread pudding of a kind
Plum pudding—Cosmos fine

Epicure
This dining of mine.

NOTHING TO SAY

I have nothing to say
The birds beat me today
In a race that was never begun

In my being I sat
With no need to chat
But to linger with sultry tongue

Not ready to learn something new
I wanted to brew or to stew
Put things together—refinish my splendor
Or polish some innards anew

Sometimes I need to be still
Shackle my hands—tie my will
Listen, that's all
To some inner call
Like nature to live without bills.

SAFE

Safe in the ordered
Safe in the neat
Safe in the symphony
Safe on retreat

Safe in well-being
Continuity is there

Poetry gives platform
To the truly aware.

S. SCOTT

JUST BE

Be happy without the sun
Be patient with the gray before day
Be part of still—Be without skills
Listen to the dove's wispy trill
Bend with the road's broken line
Sing with the fledglings new whine
Trees without light—filter still bright
Rays from their spirit—they glow

Long for a time without men
Savor androgynous—the blend
Completed the man
Stream winning his plan

Dilettante to all but the Soul.

ENDURE

Endure the trivial for profound
There's no hurry-up way to be
Slow is not slow
When you savor the glow
When you taste honey's nectar from the bee

No matter that it seems impossible to be stung.

S. SCOTT

METER IN ME

I write to remember my meter
I chat then freeze to still day
Labor in life helps me etch myself
Winter's sleep contrasts Springs of new ways

Paths for exploring all madness
All frenzy of those with wild plots
I'm directed to uncover pure nonsense

Then bask in my contrast to that.